Yasmin the Chef

written by
SAADIA FARUQI

illustrated by
HATEM ALY

PICTURE WINDOW BOOKS
a capstone imprint

To Mariam for inspiring me, and Mubashir for helping me find the right words—S.F.

To my sister, Eman, and her amazing girls, Jana and Kenzi—H.A.

Yasmin is published by Picture Window Books, a Capstone imprint
1710 Roe Crest Drive
North Mankato, Minnesota 56003
www.mycapstone.com

Library of Congress Cataloging-in-Publication Data
Names: Faruqi, Saadia, author. | Aly, Hatem, illustrator.
Title: Yasmin the chef / by Saadia Faruqi ; illustrated by Hatem Aly.
Description: North Mankato, Minnesota : Picture Window Books, [2019] | Series: Yasmin | Summary: Yasmin's family is hosting a big party, but Yasmin is worried that the traditional food her family is cooking is too spicy—so her family challenges Yasmin to come up with a dish of her own.
Identifiers: LCCN 2018046794| ISBN 9781515837848 (hardcover) | ISBN 9781515845782 (paperback) | ISBN 9781515837893 (eBook PDF)
Subjects: LCSH: Muslim girls—Juvenile fiction. | Muslim families—Juvenile fiction. | Pakistani Americans—Juvenile fiction. | Parties—Juvenile fiction. | Cooking—Juvenile fiction. | CYAC: Muslims—United States—Fiction. | Pakistani Americans—Fiction. | Family life—Fiction. | Parties—Fiction. | Cooking—Fiction.
Classification: LCC PZ7.1.F373 Yb 2019 | DDC [E]—dc23
LC record available at https://lccn.loc.gov/2018046794

Editor: Kristen Mohn
Designer: Lori Bye

Design Elements:
Shutterstock: Art and Fashion, rangsan paidaen

Printed in the United States of America.
PA49

TABLE OF CONTENTS

Chapter 1

PARTY PREP 5

Chapter 2

TOO SPICY 10

Chapter 3

YASMIN'S PARTY SURPRISE 17

CHAPTER 1

Party Prep

On Saturday morning, Yasmin woke up very excited. Tonight they were having a party! Music, friends, and best of all—staying up late! She could hardly wait.

But first there was a lot of work to be done. Cooking, cleaning, and more!

After breakfast, Baba began vacuuming the living room. "Want to help, Yasmin?" he asked.

"I'll take polish patrol!" Yasmin said.

Yasmin wiped the coffee table until it shone.

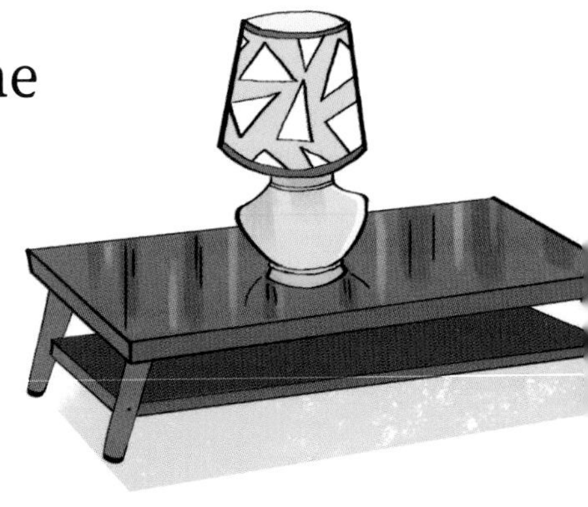

She polished the mirror till it sparkled.

And she washed the windows till they squeaked. Phew!

"Good girl!" Baba hugged Yasmin. "Let's go see if Mama needs help."

CHAPTER 2

Too Spicy

The kitchen was busy too. Yasmin looked at all the food spread out. Fruits, vegetables, chicken, rice. And lots of spices! These were the building blocks of all the dishes they would cook.

Mama clapped her hands. "Our little helper is here! Taste my fruit chaat, Yasmin."

Yasmin took a bite, then puckered her lips. "Too sour," she said.

Nani was cooking biryani. "Here, try this," she offered.

Yasmin did, then fanned her mouth. "Too spicy!" she said with a gasp.

Nana laughed. "Here, drink some chai," he suggested.

Yasmin sipped, then spit it out. “Too hot!” she yelled. The chai dribbled down her chin. “And too messy!”

“There’s nothing for me to eat,” Yasmin complained. “Why does Pakistani food have to be so spicy or sour or messy?”

Mama frowned. "Yasmin, we should be grateful for the blessings we have."

"Why don't you choose a dish to cook?" Baba said to Yasmin.

She thought. What could she cook that wasn't spicy, wasn't sour, and wasn't messy?

First she tried sandwiches. Too boring.

Then she tried a seven-layer dip. Too many layers!

Maybe a dessert? Too gooey! She threw her spoon on the counter and pouted.

Baba shook his head and sighed. "Go take a break, Yasmin," he said.

CHAPTER 3

Yasmin's Party Surprise

Yasmin moped in her room. She opened her closet to admire the sparkly shalwar kameez she would wear for the party.

She turned to her jewelry box. Which earrings would match her dress? She held up her favorite pair.

Aha! She knew what she was going to cook! She ran back down to the kitchen.

"I have an idea!" she shouted.

"I'll help," Nana offered. "You be the chef, I'll be your helper." He bowed, and Yasmin giggled.

Before long, it was evening. Yasmin came downstairs in her new kameez. The guests were just beginning to arrive.

Aunties and uncles. Cousins and friends. "What a lovely dress, Yasmin!" they all said.

The table was spread with all the food. But there was one more dish to be served.

Nana came out of the kitchen carrying Yasmin's special recipe. It wasn't spicy or sour or messy, and it was easy to eat.

"Chicken, veggie, and fruit kebab!" she announced. "A complete meal on a stick!"

Nani was the oldest, so she tasted the kebab first. "Delicious!" she cried. "Even better than my biryani."

Nana grinned. "Good work, Chef Yasmin!"

Yasmin took a bite of kebab. "Pretty good, but I think it needs just a pinch of spice," she said.

Everyone laughed.

Think About It, Talk About It

- Everyone gets frustrated sometimes. When Yasmin gets frustrated, she goes to her room to calm down. What do you do when you're upset?

- Seeing her earrings gives Yasmin an idea for a recipe. What is it about the earrings that makes her think of kebabs?

- What are some special recipes that your family makes for parties or holidays? Is there anything you would change about them if you could?

Learn Urdu with Yasmin!

Yasmin's family speaks both English and Urdu. Urdu is a language from Pakistan. Maybe you already know some Urdu words!

baba (BAH-bah)—father

biryani (bir-YAH-nee)—a dish flavored with the spices saffron or turmeric

chaat (chaht)—a spicy snack

chai (chai)—a tea drink with honey, spices, and milk

jaan (jahn)—life; a sweet nickname for a loved one

kameez (kuh-MEEZ)—a long tunic or shirt

kebab (ke-BAB)—cubes of cooked meat or vegetables, often served on a skewer

nana (NAH-nah)—grandfather on mother's side

nani (NAH-nee)—grandmother on mother's side

salaam (sah-LAHM)—hello

Pakistan Fun Facts

Yasmin and her family are proud of their Pakistani culture. Yasmin loves to share facts about Pakistan!

Location

Pakistan is on the continent of Asia, with India on one side and Afghanistan on the other.

Islamabad

PAKISTAN

Foods

Dinner often includes spicy lentils with gravy or mixed vegetables eaten with a flatbread called roti.

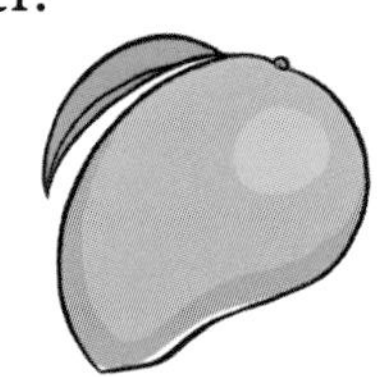

The national drink of Pakistan is sugarcane juice. The national fruit is the mango.

Language

The national language of Pakistan is Urdu, but English and several other languages are also spoken there.

سلام

(Salaam means Peace)

Make Rainbow Fruit Kebabs!

SUPPLIES:

- strawberries
- peeled orange slices
- peeled mango pieces
- peeled kiwi pieces
- blueberries
- purple grapes
- wooden skewers

STEPS:

1. Ask an adult to help you peel and cut the oranges, mango, and kiwi into bite-size pieces.

2. Place one or more of each fruit onto skewer in rainbow order: red, orange, yellow, green, blue, violet.

3. Serve to your friends and family!

About the Author

Saadia Faruqi is a Pakistani American writer, interfaith activist, and cultural sensitivity trainer previously profiled in *O Magazine*. She is author of the adult short story collection, *Brick Walls: Tales of Hope & Courage from Pakistan*. Her essays have been published in *Huffington Post*, *Upworthy*, and *NBC Asian America*. She resides in Houston, Texas, with her husband and children.

About the Illustrator

Hatem Aly is an Egyptian-born illustrator whose work has been featured in multiple publications worldwide. He currently lives in beautiful New Brunswick, Canada, with his wife, son, and more pets than people. When he is not dipping cookies in a cup of tea or staring at blank pieces of paper, he is usually drawing books. One of the books he illustrated is *The Inquisitor's Tale* by Adam Gidwitz, which won a Newbery Honor and other awards, despite Hatem's drawings of a farting dragon, a two-headed cat, and stinky cheese.

Join Yasmin on all her adventures!

Discover more at

www.capstonekids.com